William Barnes

Poems of Rural Life in Common English

William Barnes

Poems of Rural Life in Common English

ISBN/EAN: 9783337158545

Printed in Europe, USA, Canada, Australia, Japan

Cover: Foto ©Andreas Hilbeck / pixelio.de

More available books at **www.hansebooks.com**

POEMS

OF

RURAL LIFE

IN COMMON ENGLISH

BY WILLIAM BARNES

AUTHOR OF 'POEMS OF RURAL LIFE IN THE DORSET DIALECT'

LONDON

MACMILLAN AND CO.

1868

LONDON : PRINTED BY
SPOTTISWOODE AND CO., NEW-STREET SQUARE
AND PARLIAMENT STREET

PREFACE

As I think that some people, beyond the bounds of Wessex, would allow me the pleasure of believing that they have deemed the matter of my homely poems in our Dorset mother-speech to be worthy of their reading, I have written a few of a like kind, in common English; not, however, without a misgiving that what I have done for a wider range of readers, may win the good opinion of fewer.

W. BARNES.

CONTENTS

PAGE

AUTUMN 1

HOME FROM A JOURNEY 3

THE WOODSIDE ROAD 5

THE MOTHER'S DREAM 8

THE CHILD LOST 10

WHITE IN THE NIGHT 12

WHITE AND BLUE 14

WINTER COMING 16

WINTER WEATHER 18

THE BARS ON THE LANDRIDGE . . . 21

THE STREAM SIDE 23

PAGE

MELHILL FEAST 25

THE DUET 28

I AND THE DOG 30

THE SURPRISE 32

ROUND THINGS 34

A BRISK WIND 36

SHELLBROOK 37

THE WIND AT THE DOOR 39

BY THE MILL IN SPRING 41

HAPPY TIMES 43

GREEN 45

LOWSHOT LIGHT 46

THE BROKEN JUG 47

WELL TO DO 49

THE GROVE 52

WHEN WE WERE YOUNG TOGETHER . . 54

THE FIELD PATH 58

CONTENTS

PAGE

THE PARROCK 60

SING AGAIN TOGETHER 62

SEASON TOKENS 64

NOT FAR TO GO . . , , , . 66

CHANGES 68

DEADNESS OF THE COUNTRY . . . 70

THE BENCH BY THE GARDEN WALL . . 71

THE STONEN STEPS 73

ON THE HILL 76

THE OLD CLOCK 80

THE WIND UP THE STREAM 82

WORK AND WAIT 83

NO TWO DAYS ALIKE 85

SEE-SAW 87

THE SISTER AND BROTHERS 89

THE REEDS ABOUT THE POOL . . . 91

SUMMER WIND GUSTS 93

PAGE

A MATCH OF QUESTIONS 95

THE STRING TOKEN 97

SHEEP IN THE SHADE 98

CLOUDS 100

THE PRIZE WINNERS 102

WORK AFIELD 108

WHEN WE THAT HAVE CHILDREN, WERE

    CHILDREN 110

PENTRIDGE 112

SHELTER 114

BY NEIGHBOURS' DOORS 116

BETWEEN HAYMAKING AND HARVEST . . 118

HOME'S A NEST 121

ON THE ROAD 126

MOTHER OF MOTHERS 128

FALLING THINGS 131

THE MORNING MOON 134

PAGE

JOY PASSING BY 138

RIGHTING UP THE CHURCH 141

JOHN TALKING ANGRILY OF A NEIGHBOUR
BEFORE AN ECHO 143

THE SHOP OF MEAT-WARE, OR WARES TO EAT 146

WALKING HOME AT NIGHT 148

THE KNOLL 150

A WISH FULFILLED 153

AT THE DOOR 156

HILL AND DELL 159

DANIEL AND JANE 161

HOME 166

FELLOWSHIP 169

AIR AND LIGHT 172

MELDON HILL 174

SOFT SOUND 176

THE VOICE AT HOME 178

	PAGE
THE FIRESIDE CHAIRS	180
COME AND MEET ME	183
MY FORE-ELDERS	186
THE LOST LITTLE SISTER	188
BLACK AND WHITE	190
BED-RIDDEN	192
THE WINDOW	194
PLORATA VERIS LACHRYMIS	196
DO GOOD	199

AUTUMN

THE long-lighted days begin to shrink,
And flowers are thin in mead among
The late-shooting grass, that shines along
Brook upon brook, and brink by brink.

The wheat, that was lately rustling thick,
Is now up in mows that still are new ;
All yellow before the sky of blue,
Tip after tip, and rick by rick.

No starlings arise in flock on wing ;
The cuckoo has still'd his woodland sound ;
The swallow no longer wheels around,
Dip after dip, and swing by swing.

65   B

While shooters are roving round the knoll,
By wind-driven leaves on quiv'ring grass,
Or down where the sky-blue waters pass,
Fall after fall, and shoal by shoal ;

Their brown-dappled pointers nimbly trot
By russet-bough'd trees, while gun-smoke grey
Dissolves in the air of sunny day,
Reef upon reef, at shot by shot.

While now I can walk a dusty mile,
I'll take me a day while days are clear,
To find a few friends that still are dear,
Face upon face, and smile by smile.

HOME FROM A JOURNEY

BACK home on my mare I took my way,
Through hour upon hour of waning day,
Where thistles on windy ledges shook,
And aspen leaves quiver'd o'er the brook,
By slope and by level ambling on,
Till day with the sunken sun was gone,
And out in the west a 'sheet of light
Was lingering pale—pale in the night.

At last, as my mare came snorting near
My dwelling, where all things near were dear,
The apples were swung in darksome balls,
And roses hung dark beside the walls,

B 2

No cows were about the fields to low,
The fowls were at roost in sleeping row,
And only the nightingale sang high
In moongleamings pale—pale in the sky.

Within my old door my lamp was clear,
To show me the faces many and dear,
My mother's, now dimm'd by life-long care,
My wife's, as a wife's, of ten years' wear,
My children's, well shapen line by line,
One seven, one five, one three years, mine,
And one that has come before our sight,
His one moon pale—pale in the night.

THE WOODSIDE ROAD

As along by the wood of rustling beech,
And whispering pine without a breach,
I went where the gravel road did reach,
For men on their way to roam, O,
On homeward, or out from home, O.

A squire that rode a mare milkwhite,
Came on with a lady fair to sight,
All gleaming with gold, in blue bedight,
On a mettlesome bay to roam, O,
On homeward, or out from home, O.

For aught that I knew the woody ground
That then with their horses' hoofs did sound,
Was all their own land to ramble round
A half of the day, and roam, O,
On homeward, or out from home, O.

But then on a pony's tripping pace,
There came on a girl with sweetest face,
In brown, with a hood of grey, to trace
Her roadway so gay, and roam, O,
But where, aye where was her home, O?

Below at the mill, the brook's low shore?
Or else at the wheelwright's paint-streak'd door?
Or else at the dairy's well-clean'd floor?
To start in the day to roam, O,
And come before night back home, O.

I never would care for gold or land,
But only would ask her heart and hand,
And one little stable, where might stand
Her pony with hay, to roam, O,
With mine for her happy home, O.

THE MOTHER'S DREAM

I'D a dream to-night
As I fell asleep,
Oh ! the touching sight
Makes me still to weep :
Of my little lad,
Gone to leave me sad,
Aye, the child I had,
But was not to keep.

As in heaven high,
I my child did seek,
There, in train, came by
Children fair and meek,

Each in lily white,
With a lamp alight;
Each was clear to sight,
But they did not speak.

Then, a little sad,
Came my child in turn,
But the lamp he had,
Oh ! it did not burn ;
He, to clear my doubt,
Said, half turned about,
'Your tears put it out ;
Mother, never mourn.'

THE CHILD LOST

WHEN evening is closing in all round,
And winds in the dark-bough'd timber sound,
The flame of my candle, dazzling bright,
May shine full clear—full clear may shine,
But never can show my child to sight.

And warm is the bank, where boughs are still,
On timber below the windward hill,
But now, in the stead of summer hay,
Dead leaves are cast—are cast dead leaves,
Where lately I saw my child at play.

And Oh ! could I see, as may be known

To angels, my little maid full grown,

As time would have made her, woman tall,

If she had lived—if lived had she

And not have died now, so young and small.

Do children that go to heaven play ?

Are young that were gay, in heaven gay ?

Are old people bow'd by weak'ning time,

In heaven bow'd,—all bow'd in heaven ?

Or else are they all in blissful prime ?

Yes, blest with all blessings are the blest,

Their lowest of good's above our best,

So show me the highest soul you can

In shape and mind—in mind and shape

Yet far above him is heaven's man.

WHITE IN THE NIGHT

AND John, that by day is down at mill,
As soon as the night is come,
Goes out from his millgear standing still,
For home, all white in the night.

And Jenny may wear her white, as out
To town she may take her road
By day; but at dusk no more's about
Abroad, in white in the night.

For though at the brook the bridge is strong,
And white as it white can be,
That folk in the dark may not go wrong,
But see its white in the night.

And though the full moon may freely shed
Its beams upon gate and wall,
And down on the road that people tread
They fall, so white in the night.

Yet Jenny at dusk is fearful now,
Since once, in the mead alone,
She took for a ghost a sheeted cow,
Outshown in white in the night.

O Jenny, the while the moon may gleam,
I wish you would come and roam
With me, to behold the falling stream
In foam so white in the night.

For fairer than all the hues of day,
Or grass, or the sky of blue,
Or blossoms of spring that shine so gay,
Are you in white in the night.

WHITE AND BLUE

My love is of comely height and straight,
And comely in all her ways and gait,
She shows in her face the rose's hue,
And her lids on her eyes, are white on blue.

When Elemley club-men walk'd in May,
And folk came in clusters every way,
As soon as the sun dried up the dew,
And clouds in the sky were white on blue,

She came by the down with tripping walk,
By daisies and shining banks of chalk,
And brooks with the crowfoot flow'rs to strew
The sky-tinted water, white on blue;

She nodded her head as play'd the band,

She tapp'd with her foot as she did stand,

She danc'd in a reel, and wore all new

A skirt with a jacket, white and blue.

I. singled her out from thin and stout,

From slender and stout I chose her out,

And what in the evening could I do

But give her my breast-knot white and blue?

WINTER COMING

I'm glad we have wood in store awhile,
For soon we must shut the door awhile,
As winterly winds may roar awhile,
    And scatter the whirling snow.

The swallows have now all hied away,
And most of the flowers have died away,
And boughs, with their leaves all dried away,
    Are windbeaten to and fro.

Your walks in the ashtree droves are cold,
Your banks in the timber'd groves are cold,
Your seats on the garden coves are cold,
    Where sunheat did lately glow.

No rosebud is blooming red to-day,

No pink for your breast or head to-day,

O'erhanging the garden bed to-day,

    Is nodding its sweet head low.

No more is the swinging lark above,

And air overclouded dark above,

So baffles the sun's last spark above,

    That shadows no longer show.

So now let your warm cheek bloom to-night,

While fireflames heat the room to-night,

Dispelling the flickering gloom to-night,

    While winds of the winter blow.

WINTER WEATHER

When stems of elms may rise in row,
Dark brown, from hillocks under snow,
And woods may reach as black as night,
By sloping fields of cleanest white.
If shooters by the snowy rick,
Where trees are high, and wood is thick,
Can mark the tracks the game may prick,
  They like the winter weather.

Or where may spread the grey-blue sheet
Of ice, for skaters' gliding feet,
That they uplift, from side to side,
Long yards, and hit them down to slide

Or sliders, one that totters slack
Of limb; and one that's on his back;
And one upright that keeps his track,
    Have fun in winter weather.

When we at night, in snow and gloom,
May seek some neighbour's lighted room,
Though snow may show no path before
The house, we still can find the door,
And there, as round the brands may spread
The creeping fire, of cherry red,
Our feet from snow, from wind our head,
    Are warm in winter weather.

Wherever day may give our road,
By hills or hollows oversnow'd,
By windy gaps, or shelter'd nooks,
Or bridgèd ice of frozen brooks,

Still may we all, as night may come,

Know where to find a peaceful home,

And glowing fire for fingers numb

With cold, in winter weather.

THE BARS ON THE LANDRIDGE

THE bars on the timber'd ridge outspan
The gap where the shining skies may show
The people that clamber to and fro,
Woman by woman, man by man.

To strangers that once may reach the gap,
How fair is the dell beyond the ridge,
With houses and trees, and church and bridge,
Wood upon wood, and knap by knap.

Down here may be pleasant ways to rove,
But oh ! 'tis another place behind
The bars, that would take the most my mind,
Orchard by orchard, grove by grove.

When under the moon, the bars' smooth ledge,
Rubb'd up to a gloss, is bright as glass,
And shadows outmark, on dewy grass,
Rail upon rail, and edge by edge.

Then there is my way, where nightwinds sound
So softly on boughs, where lights and shades
Are playing on slopes, by hills and glades,
Tree upon tree, and mound by mound.

THE STREAM SIDE

I SAT a little while beside
A greystoned rock, the rugged brow
Of our clear pool, where waters glide
By leaning tree and hanging bough ;
In fall, when open air was cool,
And skimming .swallows left the pool,
And glades in long-cast shades did lie
Below the yet clear sky.

The leaves that through the spring were gay,
Were now by hasty winds that shook
Them wither'd off their quiv'ring spray,
All borne away along the brook,

Without a day of rest around
Their mother tree, on quiet ground.
But cast away on blast and wave,
To lie in some chance grave.

When sickness smote poor Mary low,
And sent her off her life's old ground,
To poor-house, day by day might show
Her bread, but not her friends around ;
She never fell to lie at rest,
At this old place, she liked the best,
But went as leaves off-sent by waves,
To lie in distant graves.

MELHILL FEAST

AYE up at the feast, by Melhill's brow,
So softly below the clouds in flight,
There swept on the wood, the shade and light,
Tree after tree, and bough by bough.

And there, as among the crowd, I took
My wandering way, both to and fro,
Full comely were shapes that day could show,
Face upon face, and look by look:

And there, among girls on left and right,
On one with a winsome smile, I set
My looks; and the more, the more we met
Glance upon glance, and sight by sight.

The road she had come by then was soon
The one of my paths that best I knew,
By glittering gossamer and dew,
Evening by evening, moon by moon.

First by the door of maidens fair,
As fair as the best till she is nigh,
Though now I can heedless pass them by,
One after one, or pair by pair.

Then by the orchards dim and cool,
And then along Woodcombe's timber'd side,
And then by the meads, where waters glide
Shallow by shallow, pool by pool.

And then to the house that stands alone
With roses around the porch and wall,
Where, up by the bridge, the waters fall
Rock under rock, and stone by stone.

Sweet were the hopes I found to cheer

My heart as I thought on time to come,

With one that would bless my happy home,

Moon upon moon, and year by year.

THE DUET

As late at a house I made my call,
A mother and daughter's voices rang,
In twotreble songs, they sweetly sang,
Strain upon strain, and fall by fall.

The mother was comely, still, but staid,
The daughter was young, but womantall,
As people come on to great from small,
Maid upon child, and wife from maid.

And oh ! where the mother, in the train
Of years, may have left her child alone,
With no fellow voice to match her own,
Song upon song, and strain by strain.

May Providence show the way to bring
Her voice to be mine, with me to stay,
While softly my life may wear away,
Summer by summer, spring by spring.

I AND THE DOG

As I was wont to straggle out
To your house, oh ! how glad the dog,
With low-put nose, would nimbly jog,
Along my path and hunt about ;
And his great pleasure was to run
By timber'd hedge and banky ledge,
And ended where my own begun,
At your old door and stonen floor.

And there, as time was gliding by,
With me so quick, with him so slow,
How he would look at me, and blow,
From time to time, a whining sigh,

That meant, 'Now come along the land,

With timber'd knolls, and rabbit holes,

I can't think what you have on hand,

With this young face, in this old place.'

THE SURPRISE

As there I left the road in May,
And took my way along a ground,
I found a glade with girls at play,
By leafy boughs close-hemm'd around,
And there, with stores of harmless joys,
They plied their tongues, in merry noise.
Though little did they seem to fear
So queer a stranger might be near,
Teeh-hee! Look here! Hah! ha! Look there!
And oh! so playsome, oh! so fair.

And one would dance as one would spring,
Or bob or bow with leering smiles,
And one would swing, or sit and sing,
Or sew a stitch or two at whiles,

And one skipp'd on with downcast face,

All heedless, to my very place,

And there, in fright, with one foot out,

Made one dead step and turn'd about.

Heeh, hee, oh ! oh ! ooh ! oo ! Look there !

And oh ! so playsome, oh ! so fair.

Away they scamper'd all, full speed,

By boughs that swung along their track,

As rabbits out of wood at feed,

At sight of men all scamper back.

And one pull'd on behind her heel,

A thread of cotton, off her reel,

And oh ! to follow that white clue,

I felt I fain could scamper too.

Teeh, hee, run here.   Eeh ! ee ! look there !

And oh ! so playsome, oh ! so fair.

ROUND THINGS

A FAIRY ring as round's the sun,
Beside the lea would bend its rim,
And near at hand the waves would run
Across the pond with rounded brim.
And there, by round-built ricks of hay,
By sun-heat burnt, by sunshine brown'd,
We met in merry ring, to play,
All springing on, and wheeling round.

And there, as stones we chanc'd to fling,
Swept out in flight a lofty bow,
And fell on water; ring by ring
Of waves bespread the pool below,

Beside the bridge's arch that springs

Between the banks, within the brims,

Where swung the lowly-bending swings,

On elm-tree boughs, on mossy limbs.

A BRISK WIND

THE burdock leaves beside the ledge,
The leaves upon the poplar's height,
Were blown by windblasts up on edge,
And show'd their undersides of white;
And willow trees beside the rocks,
All bent grey leaves, and swung grey boughs,
As there, on wagging heads, dark locks,
Bespread red cheeks, behung white brows.

SHELLBROOK

WHEN out by Shellbrook, round by stile and tree,
With longer days and sunny hours come on,
With spring and all its sunny showers come on,
With May and all its shining flowers come on,
How merry, young with young would meet in glee.

And there, how we in merry talk went by
The foam below the river bay, all white,
And blossom on the green-leav'd may, all white,
And chalk beside the dusty way, all white,
Where glitt'ring water match'd with blue the sky.

Or else in winding paths and lanes, along
The timb'ry hillocks, sloping steep, we roam'd;
Or down the dells and dingles deep we roam'd;
Or by the bending brook's wide sweep we roam'd
On holidays, with merry laugh or song.

But now, the frozen churchyard wallings keep
The patch of tower-shaded ground, all white,
Where friends can find the frosted mound, all white
With turfy sides upswelling round, all white
With young offsunder'd from the young in sleep.

THE WIND AT THE DOOR

As daylight darken'd on the dewless grass,
There still, with no one come by me,
To stay awhile at home by me,
Within the house, now dumb by me,
I sat me still as eveningtide did pass.

And there a windblast shook the rattling door,
And seem'd, as wind did moan without,
As if my love alone without,
And standing on the stone without,
Had there come back with happiness once more.

I went to door, and out from trees, above
My head, upon the blast by me,
Sweet blossoms there were cast by me,
As if my love had pass'd by me,
And flung them down, a token of her love.

Sweet blossoms of the tree where now I mourn,
I thought, if you did blow for her,
For apples that should grow for her,
And fall red-ripe below for her,
Oh! then how happy I should see you kern.

But no. Too soon my fond illusion broke,
No comely soul in white like her,
No fair one, tripping light, like her,
No wife of comely height like her,
Went by, but all my grief again awoke.

BY THE MILL IN SPRING

WITH wind to blow, and streams to flow,

To flow along the gravel stone,

The waves were bright, the cliffs were white,

Were white before the evening sun,

Where shaken sedge would softly sigh,

As we, with windblown locks, went by.

As lambs would swing their tails, and spring;

And spring about the ground chalk white;

The smoke was blue, above the yew;

The yew beside your house in sight;

And wind would sing with sullen sound,

Against the tree beside the mound;

Where down at mill, the wheel was still,
Was still, and dripp'd with glitt'ring tears,
With dusty poll, up lane would stroll,
The miller's man with mill-stunn'd ears;
While weakly-wailing wind would swim,
By ground with ivied elm-trees dim.

My work and way may fail or fay,
Or fay as days may freeze or glow,
I'll try to bear my toil or care,
Or care, with either friend or foe,
If, after all, the evening tide
May bring me peace, where I abide.

HAPPY TIMES

How smoothly then did run my happy days,
When things to charm my mind and sight were nigh ;

The glitt'ring brook, that wander'd round my home,
With rock-shot foam, downfalling white, was nigh ;

And glossy-wingèd rooks, above the grove,
Off-sweeping round their tree, in flight, were nigh.

And daws about the castle's ruggèd walls,
And ivy-hooded tower's height, were nigh.

A bower outhollow'd in a hedge of yew,
Would yield me shelter'd rest, when night was nigh,

And in the dusk of moonshades, near the door,
My playsome children, skipping light, were nigh.

And there I never met a grief half way,
In thinking ev'ry day a blight was nigh.

But found it best, with thankfulness and care,
To feel that He that is our might, was nigh.

GREEN

OUR summer way to church did wind about

The cliff, where ivy on the ledge was green.

Our summer way to town did skirt the wood,

Where shining leaves, in tree and hedge, were green.

Our summer way to milking in the mead,

Was on by brooks, where flutt'ring sedge was green.

Our homeward ways all gathered into one,

Where moss upon the roofstone's edge was green.

LOWSHOT LIGHT

As I went eastward ere the sun had set,
His yellow light on bough by bough was bright.

And there, by buttercups beside the hill,
Below the elmtrees, cow by cow, was bright.

While, after heavy-headed horses' heels,
With slowly-rolling wheels, the plough was bright.

And up among the people, on the sides,
One lovely face, with sunny brow, was bright.

And aye, for that one face, the bough, and cow,
And plough, in my sweet fancy, now are bright.

THE BROKEN JUG

JENNY AND TOM

(Tom idly swings about Jenny's jug, and breaks
it against a stone)

J. As if you could not leave the jug alone !

Now you have smack'd my jug ;

Now you have whack'd my jug ;

Now you have crack'd my jug,

Against the stone.

T. The jug was crack'd before, unknown to you:

So don't belie the stone ;

It scarce went nigh the stone,

It just went by the stone,

And broke in two.

J. Oh ! crack'd before ! no ! that was sound enough,

From back to lip was sound,

To stand or tip was sound,

To hold or dip, was sound.

    Don't talk such stuff.

T. How high then must I take its price to reach ?

I'd buy some more as good ;

I'd buy a score as good ;

I'd buy a store as good ;

    For twopence each.

J. Indeed ! when stonen jugs are sold so dear !

No, there's a tap for lies ;

And there's a slap for lies ;

And there's a rap for lies,

    About your ear.

T. Oh ! there are pretty hands ! a little dear !

WELL TO DO

As wind might blow along the snow,
By shelter'd nooks, and hollow caves,
By icy eaves, and frosty leaves,
And streams too hard to run in waves,
No inn-board then, in swinging slack,
And creaking shrill, would keep me back,
Would call me back, by creaking shrill,
From home and you, beyond the hill,
 , Though we were well to do.

When down before our porchèd door,
The moonshade of the house might lie,
Our room would show a ruddy glow
To muffled people passing by,

For we had flames before our feet,
And on our board, both meal and meat;
Both meal and meat upon our board,
Without a stint, could we afford,
   So well were we to do.

When snow was deep, for our few sheep,
And made their whitest wool look brown,
And cold-pinched cows, below white boughs,
Had no warm ground to lay them down,
Then I'd a roof for ev'ry head,
For ev'ry hide a strawen bed,
A strawen bed for ev'ry hide,
And cribs of hay all fill'd with pride,
   So well was I to do.

When clad anew, from crown to shoe,
The children walk'd with prouder pace,
And you might tell, or only spell,
Of what would suit your shape or face,

And you came out, and look'd so fine,

I felt quite proud to call you mine,

To call you mine I felt quite proud,

Before our friends, or in a crowd,

   When we were well to do.

THE GROVE

'TWAS there in summer down the grove,
Where I and long-lost friends would rove,
Where then the gravelbedded brook,
O'ershaded under hanging boughs,
On-trickled round the quiet nook,
Or lay in pools for thirsty cows.

And here are still the stones we trod,
In stepping o'er the stream, dryshod,
And here are leaves that lie all dead,
About the lofty-headed-tree,
Where leaves then quiver'd overhead,
All playfully alive as we.

While now, by moonlight, nightwinds keen,

May shake the ivy, ever green,

By this old wall, and hemlocks dry

May rattle by the leafless thorn,

I still can fancy people by

That I have lost, to live forlorn.

WHEN WE WERE YOUNG TOGETHER

JOHN AND FRIEND

J. WHEN we, all friends, in manhood's prime,

Did meet, work free, with weather fine ;

And you had made, at evening time,

Your work-day good, as I had mine.

Then one would call, as he might come,

To fetch another out from home :

'Come out a while with me.'

'Aye, I shall soon be free.'

'How long have I to wait ?'

'Why, I am coming straight.'

Fr. Aye, aye, 'twas so, we did, I know,

When we were young together.

J. While summer days might slowly run,
    Through noons of shrunken shades, and heat,
    And we, well-brown'd below the sun,
    Might meet, and call as we might meet :
  ' Hallo ! why you but seldom come
    For me.' ' Nor you for me at home.'
  ' Well, where's your road to night?
  ' Where you should go by right'
  ' Shall I be welcome there ? '
  ' To one, I'd nearly swear.'

Fr. Aye, aye, like that, we used to chat,
    When we were young together.

J. Then we, with many dear old names,
    Would meet within some neighbour's door,
    And man and maid, in merry games,
    Would spring and scuff about the floor.
    If one might speak a little tart,
    Another's answer was as smart.

'With whom are you to go ?

'Here face to face in row.'

'Here, now we'll dance a reel,'

'Well foot it, toe and heel.'

Fr. Aye, there we danced,

And hopp'd and pranced,

When we were young together.

J. Then we in all our pride, would try

Which man could run, or leap the best,

Or lift the greatest weight, or shy

A pebble truer than the rest.

'Who'll walk along these narrow poles ?'

'Not you, my lad, with your splay soles,'

'Now, you can't hit that stone.'

'I can, *whee-it.* Well done !

'Well, you can't clear the brook.'

'Oh, can't I then ? You look.'

Fr. And down he dash'd, as water splash'd,

When we were young together.

In summer time we went to take

Our picnic, by the castle walls,

And play'd our games beside the lake,

Where swam the swans, by waterfalls ;

And there, for merry pranks did crawl,

About the trees, or broken wall.

' Here, see how high am I.'

' Well here am I, as high.'

' You can't climb down, old boy.'

' I can, I'll bet '—' Heigh ! hoy ! '

Fr. And down he fell, you need not tell,

When we were young together.

THE FIELD PATH

HERE sounded words of dear old folk,
  Of this dear ground,
  Where ivy wound
About this ribbèd oak.
And still their words, their words now gone,
Are dear to me that linger on.

And here, as comely forms would pass,
  Their shades would slide
  Below their side,
Along the flow'ry grass.
And now, their shades, their shades now gone,
Still hallow ground they fell upon.

But could they come where then they stroll'd,

    However young

    Might sound their tongue,

Their shades would show them old.

So sweet are shades, the shades now shown,

The shades of trees they all have known.

These ashen poles that shine so tall,

    Are still too young

    To have upsprung

In days when I was small ;

But you, stout oak, you, oak so stout,

Were here when my first moon ran out.

THE PARROCK

WITHIN the parrock in a nook,
By high-shot elm-trees all around
Its sides, where upper tree-boughs shook
In wind that hardly sank to ground,
    By bough, by cow,
With pail and stool, when air was cool,
    We sat in parrock, in the nook.

And there, as evening shades might fall,
From elms along the western rank.
Or else, as moonlight, from the tall-
Stemm'd trees, might reach the eastern bank,
    By ledge, by hedge,
We then would walk, or sit and talk,
    Within the parrock in a nook.

Where bright by day the grass may look,

Where cool the shade may fall at noon,

Where dark is yet our shady nook,

Or pale the ground below the moon,

    By tump, by hump,

I still would go, with one I know,

    Within the parrock, in a nook.

SING AGAIN TOGETHER

SINCE now, once more beside this mound,
We friends are here below the limes,
Come, let us try if we can sound
A song we sang in early times.

When out among the hay in mead,
Or o'er the fields, or down the lane,
Our Jenny's voice would gaily lead
The others, chiming strain by strain.

When roses' buds are all outblown,
The lilies' cups will open white,
When lilies' cups, at last, are flown,
The later pinks unfold to sight.

We learnt good songs that came out new,
But now are old among the young,
And, after we are gone, but few
Will know the songs that we have sung.

So let us sing another rhyme
On this old mound in summer time.

SEASON TOKENS

THE shades may show the time of day,
And flowers, how summer wanes away.

Where thyme on turfy banks may grow,
Or mallows, by the laneside ledge,
About the blue-barr'd gate, may show
Their grey-blue heads, beside the hedge,
Or where the poppy's scarlet crown
May nod by clover, dusky red,
Or where the field is ruddy brown,
By brooks, with shallow-water'd bed.

The shades may show the time of day,
And flow'rs, how summer wanes away.

Or, where the light of dying day,

May softly shine against the wall,

Below the sloping thatch, brown-grey,

Or over pale-green grass, may fall,

Or where, in fields that heat burns dry,

May show the thistle's purple studs,

Or beds of dandelions ply

Their stems with yellow fringèd buds.

There shades may show the time of day,

And flowers, how summer wanes away.

NOT FAR TO GO

As upland fields were sunburnt brown,
And heat-dried brooks were running small,
And sheep were gather'd, panting all,
Below the hawthorn on the down;
The while my mare, with dipping head,
Pull'd on my cart, above the bridge;
I saw come on, beside the ridge,
A maiden, white in skin and thread,
And walking, with an elbow load,
The way I drove, along my road.

As there, with comely steps, up hill
She rose by elm-trees, all in ranks,
From shade to shade, by flow'ry banks,
Where flew the bird with whistling bill,

I kindly said, 'Now won't you ride,

This burning weather, up the knap?

I have a seat that fits the trap,—

And now is swung from side to side.'

'O no,' she cried, 'I thank you, no.

I've little farther now to go.'

Then, up the timber'd slope, I found

The prettiest house, a good day's ride

Would bring you by, with porch and side,

By rose and jessamine well bound,

And near at hand, a spring and pool,

With lawn well sunn'd and bower cool :

And while the wicket fell behind

Her steps, I thought, if I would find

A wife, I need not blush to show,

I've little farther now to go.

CHANGES

AND oh ! what changes we all know,
Long years can bring in one small place,
In names and shapes, from face to face,
As souls will come and souls will go :
And here, where hills have all stood fast,
While babes have come and men have pass'd,
The wind-stream softly seems to sigh,
' Man's lifetime glides away as I.'

The child may open here his eyes,
Long miles away to live a man,
The mother here may end her span
Of life, where no dear daughter lies.

CHANGES

As time steals on, fiom day to day,
And nothing stands at one same stay,
The wind-blast softly seems to sigh,
' Man's lifetime glides away as I.'

As clapper-sounded bells ring fast,
They tell the moments out, and clocks
That slowly sound by knocks on knocks,
May tell how daily hours have pass'd ;
In Sunday chimes a week is fled,
In Easter knells a year is dead,
And airy bell-sounds seem to say,
Like us man's lifetime glides away.

DEADNESS OF THE COUNTRY

O NO, 'twas lifeless here, he said,
To him the place seem'd all but dead,
Stone-dead, he said, but why so dead,
On lands with chirping birds on wing,
And rooks on high, with blackbirds nigh,
And swallows wheeling round in ring,
And fish to swim, where waters roam,
By bridge and rock to fall in foam.

THE BENCH BY THE GARDEN WALL

As day might cool, and in the pool,
The shaded waves might ripple dim,
We used to walk, or sit in talk,
Below the limetree's leaning limb,
Where willows' drooping boughs might fall
Around us, near the garden wall.

Where children's heads on evening beds,
In dull-ear'd sleep were settled sound,
The moon's bright ring would slowly spring,
From down behind the woody mound,
With light that slanted down on all
The willows nigh the garden wall.

By roof-eaves spread up over head,
There clung the wren's brown nest of hay,
And wind would make the ivy shake,
And your dark locks of hair to play,
As you would tell the news of all
The day, beside the garden wall.

The while might run, the summer sun,
On high, above the green-tree'd land,
Few days would come, for jaunts from home,
And none without some work on hand,
Yet we enjoy'd at eveningfall,
Our bench beside the garden wall.

Our flow'rs would blow, our fruit would grow,
To hang in air, or lie on ground,
Our bees would hum, or go and come
By small-door'd hives, well hackled round;
All this we had, and over all
Our bench beside the garden wall.

THE STONEN STEPS

A MAN AND HIS FRIEND

M. THESE stonen steps that stand so true
With tread on tread, a foot-reach wide,
Have always climb'd the sloping side
Of this steep ledge, for me and you ;
Had people built the steps before
They turn'd the arch of our old door ?
Were these old stairs laid down by man,
Before the bridge's archèd span ?
Did workmen set these stones so trim
Before they built the spire so slim ?

Fr. Ah ! who can tell when first—aye who,—
These steps first bore a shoe.

M. And here, beside the sloping hump,

From stone to stone with faces flat,

The littlefooted children pat,

And heavy-booted men-folk clump;

But which the last may beat a shoe,

On these old stones, shall I or you?

Which little boy of mine shall climb

These well-worn steps, the last in time?

Which girl, childquick, or womanslow,

Shall walk the last these stones in row?

Fr. Aye, who among us now can know

Who last shall come or go?

M. The road leads on, below these blocks

To yonder springhead's stony cove,

And Meldon Hall; and elm-tree grove,

And mill, beside the foamy rocks,

And up these well-worn blocks of stone

I came when I first ran alone,

The stonen stairs beclimb'd the mound,

Ere father put a foot to ground,

'Twas up the steps his father came,

To make his mother change her name.

Fr. Aye, who can ever tell what pairs

Of feet once trod the stairs?

ON THE HILL

HUSBAND AND WIFE

H. WHY 'tis nice on the hill, at the time of the year
When the summer is in, and the weather is clear,
When the flow'rs at our feet are all blossoming gay,
And the fields down below us are grey with the hay,
Hallo ! why 'tis steep, and you pant. Will you stop ?

    And look down around,

    At rest on the ground,

    Where thyme is outspread

    In a bed, on the mound.

Over yonder, how glittering sway the treetops,
All glowing with sunlight that shoots by the copse,

Where bluebells in white-clouded May-time bestrew

The wood-shelter'd glade in a sheet of pale blue.

You are cold in the shoulders, then, Put on your

. shawl.

W. There Brown's folk all guide

Their new boat for a ride.

You may see their oars play

With the spray at the side.

H. Out there are the hawthorns, where blossoms now

fade,

Some here, and some there, with less shelter than

shade,

The old ones, like fathers, now ready to fall ;

The younger, like children, from greater to small ;

And some are as prim as a man in his prime.

And some with their shroud

That west winds have bow'd,

As eastward they set

With their wet-shedding cloud.

W. Well now here we are, on the uppermost ground,

    Where the thyme-bedded hillocks are swelling so round,

    But what place is this with the banks lying low,

    And the big mossy flintstones in straight-reaching row.

H. Why here, by the tale that poor father would tell,

        A beacon did stand,

        To light with a brand,

        And call men to blows

        If their foes were to land.

    There's a cloud o'er the lowland, that floats at our

        height,

    With its shadow o'ersweeping the ground in its flight,

W. Now it climbs o'er the tow'r, now o'ershadows the

        boughs,

    Now it leaps o'er the stream, now it darkens the cows,

    'Tis now on the rook'ry, and now on the ricks,

        And now comes to catch

        Up our own little hatch,

        And shade from the sun

        The red tun on our thatch.

W. There's a man on a horse, oh ! he spurs him well on,

    Is somebody ill then ? or where is he gone ?

    There's a maid by the buttercups there,—and 'tis who ?

    Jane Hine I can tell by her skirt of pale blue ;

    And now she is slipping along by the slope,

        And now she looks round

        In a fright, at the sound,

        Of the bull that is blaring

        And tearing the ground.

THE OLD CLOCK

THAT old clock's face yet keeps its place,
And wheels its hands around,
His bob still swings, his bell still rings,
As when I heard his sound,
On leaving home so long ago,
And left him ticking, ticking slow.

No rust yet clogs its catching cogs,
To keep its wheels all still,
No blow e'er fell to crack his bell,
That hourly ringles shrill.
I wish my life were guided on
As true as that old clock has gone.

Who now may wind his chain, untwin'd

In running out his hours,

Or make a gloss to shine across

His door, with golden flow'rs,

Since he has sounded out the last

Still hours our dear good mother pass'd.

THE WIND UP THE STREAM

THE shaded river ran below
A ledge, with elms that stood in row,
By leafy ivy-stems intwin'd,
In light that shot from rind to rind;
And winds that play'd, now brisk, now slack,
Against the stream, were driving back
The running waves, and made them seem
To show an upward-flowing stream:
As man, while hope beguiles him, thinks
His life is rising while it sinks.

WORK AND WAIT

HUSBAND AND WIFE

H. THE sweet'ning fruit that fall shall bring
    Is now a bud within its rind;
    The nest the bird shall build in spring
    Is now in moss and grass untwin'd;
    The summer days will show us, hung
    On boughs, the fruit and nest of young.
    I waited on, through time and tide,
    Till I could house you here, my bride.

W. If wedlock bonds in heaven are bound,
    Then what's our lot will all come round.

H. My new-built house's brick-red side
    A few years since was clay unfound;
    My reeden roof, outslanting wide,
    Was yet in seed, unsprung from ground.

And now no house on Woodcombe land

Is put much better out of hand

Than this, that I, through time and tide,

Was bent to build for you to guide.

W. I'll try with heart, and hand, and head,

That you shall speed as you have sped.

H. A few years since my wheels, unmade,

Were living timber, under bark,

And my new ploughshare's grey-blue blade

Was ore deep lying in the dark;

But now I have my gear, and now

Have bought two mares to haul or plough.

I waited on, in careful mood,

For stock to win our livelihood.

W. Aye 'work and wait's' the wisest way,

For 'work and wait' will win the day.

NO TWO DAYS ALIKE

Aye, no two days, in all the year,
May fall alike in ev'ry way;
Alike in clouds that skies may show,
In all their glowing dyes,
Alike in winds, as low or high,
Or east or west, or wet or dry.

Alike in birds, that gripe the bark,
Or pipe on boughs, as leaved or bare,
Alike in cows, by mound or tree,
Dispers'd about the ground;
Below a moon, as thin a bow,
Or full, with stars as high or low.

Alike in ev'ry face, to take
Its place, with all its looks again,
And tongues to speak the same kind words,
Or call again each name.
Alike in trodden path, and flow'r
Below the feet, the selfsame hour.

If night can never fall to men
With all a foreday show'd their minds,
Then how shall merry cheer outlast
The many-nighted year;
Or why should time no more fulfil
Our hope for change to good from ill?

SEE-SAW

A HOUSEWIFE TO A NEIGHBOUR

H. So you are out of tea, then, quite,
And out of candle for the night?
N. And must be till the flood is down,
And I can go again to town.

H. Come in, then, you shall have your share
Of anything that I can spare;
It would be hard if my good friends
Did me good turns, without amends.
At *see-saw, see-saw,* I and you
Would always make the fellow two.

N. As we had pull'd the uppermost
      Grey rail, out clear of post and post,
      And on the middle bar would lay
      Its even-weighted ends ; to play
      At see-saw, high, with springy toes,
      And see-saw, low, with springy blows.

H. And, so as you lift me, I'll try
      To lift up you, if I am high ;
      Some evil day, if I let you
      Fall down, why, I may tumble too.

THE SISTER AND BROTHERS

Joe. COME out to see the glowworms, Do,

As thick as blossoms on a bough.

S. O no ; the grass is wet with dew,

And I have put on slippers now.

Here's Tom.

Where is it he comes from ?

Tom. The nightingale's by Woodcombe bog :

Come down to hear it over hill.

S. No, 'tis too far, and full of fog

Out there ; I shall but catch a chill.

Here's Bill, head foremost.

What's his will ?

Bill.   The Lincham bells are up full swing
      And ringing peals.   Come up the knoll.

S.   And ringing peals ! Why they can't ring
      There now, they are but fit to toll.
      Well done.

              Here's Tom again, full run.

Tom.   John Hine is by his garden wall,
      And playing on his clarinet.

S.   How I am teazed among you all !
      I s'pose you'll have me out a bit.

THE REEDS ABOUT THE POOL

WE children, hot at work, here built
Our hut for childhood play, of beds
Of reeds, all wound with sticks, to screen
From wind our little glossy heads ;
And there we set, to shoot the wet,
Our roof of reeds, about the pool.

As deep and shoal might sleep below
A shell of ice, in winter tide,
We there, with tott'ring heads, would drive
Our toes along the grated slide,
With many a sprawl, in many a fall,
Within the reeds about the pool.

There men would draw the water out,
As dry as all their pails could dip,
And then would dip their hands about,
Well daub'd with mud, from toe to hip,
As they might feel the slipp'ry eel,
Within the reeds about the pool.

And there the nightingale would sound
Her note, while other birds were still,
As water show'd the light the moon
Might shed on stream, and mead, and hill,
On boughs aloft, while rustled soft
The reeds that sway'd about the pool.

And still below the shady mound
That leans by timber-trees in ranks,
There runs the brook that up the dell
Outbreaks, to come by winding banks
Down here to us, to open wide
A pool, with reeds about its side.

SUMMER WIND GUSTS

How gaily fair the flow'ry land
In glare of summer light would look,
With roaming cows to stalk by meads,
Or brows of fields, beside the brook;
As wind would whirl and curl,
And wildly drive about our heads
White drifts of dust, in peck by peck,
Or else would spring with hay in meads,
And fling it up about our neck,

   In playing round the summer ground.

As water flow'd below our feet,
And show'd our shades in line and hue,
A gust awoke in sudden flight,
And broke them up away from view,

In playsome whirl and curl;
And while, with darksome shade, the sun
Once mark'd our shapes within the glade,
The wind brought by a shading cloud
On high, and hid them, shade by shade,
  In streaming soft, with clouds aloft.

The winds may roll the thistledown
By knoll or mead, in summer light,
Or else may blow, in winter days,
The snow against my blinded sight,
With many a whirl and curl;
Or under rock or smooth-wall'd tow'r
May mock my song, or sound my call,
Or sway, through hours of lonesome night,
My flow'rs in bloom, by ground or wall,
  Onstreaming soft, and blowing oft.

A MATCH OF QUESTIONS

JOHN AND THOMAS

J. WHERE the stream of the river may bound,
All in foam, over block upon block,
Of grey stone, shall we say that the sound
Is the sound of the stream or the rock?

T. Where the black-spotted bean-bloom is out,
As we talk of the smell, do we mean
That the sweetness that wavers about
Is the smell of the wind or the bean?

J. Where the sunlight that plays off and on,
In the brook-pool, may dazzle your sight,
Would you say that the bow-neckèd swan
Is in gleams of the pool, or the light?

T. When your head should have met, in the night,
　　With the door, and be ready to split,
　　Would you say, if you wished to be right,
　　'Twas the head or the door that was hit?

J. When the heart may leap high at the sight
　　Of the dwelling of some belov'd face,
　　Shall we take it, that all our delight
　　Is a charm of the face, or the place?

T. When a pretty girl's father, one night,
　　Set the dog at a youth, that would scan
　　Her abode, should we think the poor wight
　　Put to flight, by the dog or the man?

J. Ah! you only can turn it to fun.
T. And he only could learn how to run.

THE STRING TOKEN

'If I am gone on, you will find a small string'—
Were her words—'on this twig of the oak by the
    spring.'
Oh! gay are the new-leavèd trees, in the spring,
Down under the height, where the skylark may sing;
And welcome in summer are tree-leaves that meet
On wide-spreading limbs, for a screen from the heat;
And fair in the fall-tide may flutter the few
Yellow leaves of the trees that the sky may shine
    through.
But welcomer far than the leaves, is the string
On the twig of the oak by the spring.

SHEEP IN THE SHADE

In summer time, I took my road
From stile to stile, from ground to ground,
The while the cloudless sunshine glowed,
On down and mead, by sun-heat browned,
Where slowly round a wide-bent bow
The stream wound on, with water low :
In hopeful hours that glided on,
With me in happiness now gone.

And there, below the elm-tree shroud,
Where shaded air might cooler swim,
There lay a quickly-panting crowd
Of sheep, within the shadow's rim,

That glided slowly, on and on,

Till there they lay, with shadow gone.

And oh! that happy hours should glide

Away so soon, with time and tide.

CLOUDS

Onriding slow, at lofty height,
Were clouds in drift along the sky,
Of purple blue, and pink, and white,
In pack and pile, upreaching high,
For ever changing, as they flew,
Their shapes from new again to new.

And some like rocks, and towers of stone,
Or hills, or woods, outreaching wide;
And some like roads, with dust upblown
In glittering whiteness off their side,
Outshining white, again to fade,
In figures made to be unmade.

So things may meet, but never stand,

In life; they may be smiles or tears:

A joy in hope, and one in hand;

Some grounds of grief, and some of fears;

They may be good, or may be ill,

But never long abiding still.

THE PRIZE WINNERS

SPEAKERS.—The Teller (*T.*) of the Cleveburn winners in games at another village. The Teller's Chorus (*T. C.*) of two or three young men come home with him. The Full Chorus (*F. C.*) of village hearers.

T. OLD CLEVEBURN for ever ! Go, ringers, and turn

The brown tower door on its greystonen durn,

And take every man in his uphanging hands

The ropes' twisted strands——

F. C. What now, then ? what now ?

T. And ring up a peal ; for you ought to be proud

Of your brothers, and sons. Come and cheer them aloud ;

For the men of old Cleveburn will bring from the
   feast
Three prizes at least.

T. C.   Now guess for the three.

T.   'Tis spryfooted Jim, and 'tis broadshoulder'd Joe,
And young Willy that jumps like a winglifted
   crow,
By the tall ashen tree.

F. C.   Here's a clap for each chap, then ; hurrah!

T.   There Jim, with five others, went off with a bound
From the line, on the grass ; like a hare-hunting
   hound,
With outreaching breast ; and with looks that no
   face
Could turn from the race.

F. C.   Well done, Jim! well done!

T.   And they shot through the tree-shades, like birds
              on the wing,
          And could hear but one gush of the rock-leaping
              spring ;
          And a rook they outstripp'd, with their flight on
              the ground,
          Turned hopeless around.

T. C.   And spryfooted Jim
          Came in quickly-panting, with red-blooming face,
          The first by a nose—ay a head—ay a pace,
          The sleekest of limb.

F. C.   Here's a cheer, he should hear, then ; hurrah !

T.   Then on came the light-footed jumpers, to bound,
          For height in the air, and for length on the ground ;
          And they sprang with their legs to their thighs
              gather'd back,
          Till they pitch'd, falling slack.

F. C.   Well done, then ! well done !

T. And they mark'd a long air-track, and settled as
tight

As a rook in a field, from a few yards of flight ;

Though one would pitch backward, and one pitch
ahead,

And one with firm head.

T. C. But, in jumping, young Bill

Outstripped all the crew ; and his heel smothered
low

The head of a flow'r that had no other blow,

From a foot by the hill.

F. C. Good strokes, merry folks, then ; hurrah !

T. Then on came the boats, up the river's broad face,

Each ploughing a furrow of foam, in its race,

While the oarsmen fell back, and their two oars
would turn

To sweep back astern,

F. C.   Well done, then ! well done !

T.   Or else as the down-leaning rowers would bow,

Their oars flew ahead for new water to plough ;

As they floated by willow, or ivy-hung rock,

Or by herd, or by flock.

T. C.   But broadshoulder'd Joe,

With the heat on his brow, and an oar in each fist,

Rush'd in with the first of the crews on the list

That did row.

F. C.   Well done, every son ! then, hurrah !

T.   So let Will leap the brook, where no bridge may

be placed,

And not stay to climb over bars in his haste,

But over them bound, ay, and over them fly,

In his shoes ankle high.

F. C.   Well done, Will ! well done !

T.   And Jim run the fields of old Cleveburn, a match;

For a hound in full run, or the hare he would

catch,

And Joe row his boat up the stream, with a

weight

Of the girls for a freight.

T. C.   Ay ; jump, run, and row ;

For who among us is ashamed to belong

To Cleveburn, with men that are spry and are

strong

As Bill, Jim, and Joe?

F. C.   It is done ; they have won ; then, hurrah !

WORK AFIELD

HUSBAND AND WIFE

H. ALL day below, tall trees in row,

    In trimming boughs, that kept me warm ;

The white chips played, about my blade,

    In wood that baffled wind and storm ;

No voice did rise, but sounds of cows,

And birds' thin cries, by tangled boughs,

Where leaves down-shed from beeches red,

    Had fallen o'er the grassy bank,

Or else lay down, all withered brown,

    By elm-trees up in stately rank.

W. I'm sure you must be glad enough
    To be in warmth, with wind so rough;
    And glad to leave the chirping birds,
    To hear a tongue that talks with words.

W. When you shall sway at mowing hay,
    And elm-tree groves shall all be dried,
    And Stour below shall wander slow
    With glittering waves at eventide;
    Or corn in load, on red-wheel rims,
    Shall grind the road, or brush tree-limbs,
    The while the bell in tower may tell,
    'Tis time to shut your day's work out,
    And you may flag, and hardly drag
    Your labour-wearied limbs about.
    Why then, before the fall is come,
    Your little girl will hail you home.

H. Ay, I shall leave the sounds of birds,
    To hear Poll's prattling tongue, with words.

WHEN WE THAT HAVE CHILDREN,
WERE CHILDREN.

Ah ! where the hedge across the hill
With high-grown boughs did grow,
And ashes' limbs were widely spread,
With up-grown tips, above our head,
And out and in, with broken brink,
The brook ran on below.

As wind-blown leaves were driven dry
In drifts, we hastened through
The grove, where frost yet lingered white,
In shadows cast by winter light,
To reach our homely house ere night
Should hide our path from view.

As you might touch, with nimble tips

Of toes, the ground, so fleet

In whirling wind, would gather strong

Behind the frock you swept along .

The ruddy leaves, and lift them up

In leaps, behind your feet.

But now, again, in treading trim

Our track, the same old way,

We both walk on with slower gait,

On feet that bear our full-grown weight,

And leave our little children's toes

To leap, and run in play.

PENTRIDGE

(1) How happy the evenings, when I, in my pride,
Here walked on with you and some more at my side,
Your cousin, and Harry, and Mary that died.

(2) In summer with dew.

(1) As lively as larks, down the slope of the hill,
We tripp'd on to Pentridge, where down at the mill,
The Stour-driven wheel is again standing still.

(2) In summer with dew, where cows were at rest,
  And over the water, and over the grass,
  And over the road, that again we shall pass,
Blew softly a wind from the west.

(1) The house that, at Pentridge, then yielded its smoke,
Was mossy 's an elm, but as firm as an oak,
To shelter the glossy-haired heads of its folk,

(2) In summer with dew.

(1) But now, where the wall-blossom hung, is no wall,

And now, where the cattle were fed, is no stall,

And now, on the ground of the house-floor, may fall

In summer the dew, (2) where blossom is white,

And over the rushes, and over the sedge,

And over the path from the river's green edge,

Blows softly the wind of the night.

(1) And now, if we go to the mill down below

The hill, where the slow-gliding waters yet flow,

Or the fields where in boyhood I went to and fro,

In summer with dew :

Whereto ? Of the house we shall find not a trace.

To whom ? Of my kindred we find not a face.

For what ? For my business is far from the place,

In summer with dew, (2) and swallows on wing,

While on by the stile, and along by the bank,

And on by the lane, with the elm-trees in rank,

Blows softly the wind of the spring.

I

SHELTER

As lately I wound up the slope, along under
The trees, where the cows lay asleep all asunder,
The moon seem'd, above me, to float in cloud-streamings,
As over its face they would flit in its beamings,

    And I went between
      The two woods in the gloom,
    When may-leaves were green,
      And the thorn was in bloom.

The wind, as along in the lea I did wander,
Blew loud over head, to sound lower out yonder,
And sweep by the roof that might hide the dull sleeper,
Or shut up the much-tossing head of the weeper.

Till once more his sight

   Might behold, in the grounds,

Dewy morning's red light,

   And should hear the day's sounds.

And there, as the wind-blasts might sweep on, and ramble

By hedges, and swing in a swoop on the bramble,

And down in the mead round the ricks they were raving,

While blossomy boughs, on the rocks were all waving.

   I joyed in the blast

      With its high-swelling roar,

   While the trees that I pass'd

      Were all guides to my door.

BY NEIGHBOURS' DOORS

As up on trees' high limbs,
'The western sunshine glowed,
And down by river brims
The wind-blown ripples flowed,
There we did seek the tun
Where evening smoke rose grey,
While dells begun to miss the light of day.

The mother-holden child,
Before the gate, would spring,
And crow, and struggle wild
At sight of birds on wing;
And home-bound men would shout
And make their game, before
The girls come out in clusters at the door.

Then we'd a door where all

Might gather to their rest,

When pale-beam'd stars might fall

Above the red-sky'd west,

But now, from that old door

We all have taken flight,

And some no more can tell the day from night.

BETWEEN

HAYMAKING AND HARVEST

(JOHN AND HIS FRIEND)

J. THE sunsped hours, with wheeling shades,
Have warm'd, for month on month, the glades,
Till now the summer wanes;
Though shadows quiver down below
The boughs, that lofty elm-trees throw
    Across the dusty lanes;

F.   and docks,
With ruddy stems, have risen tall
Beside the cow-forsaken stall,
    All free of hoofy hocks.

J. Along the swath with even side,   •

The meadow flow'rs have fall'n and died,

And wither'd, rustling dry ;

And in between the hay-wale's backs,

The waggon wheels have cut their tracks,

With loads of hay built high,

F.   and bound,

And ev'ry rick with peakèd crown,

Is now down-toned to yellow brown,

And sunburnt, two-thirds round.

J. The clouds now ride at upper height,

Above the barley yellow white ;

By lane and hedge ; along

The fields of wheat, that ripen red,

And slowly reel, with giddy head,

In wind that streams full strong,

F.   by copse,

And grass-field, where the cows lie down

Among the bent-grass, ruddy brown,

And thistles' purple tops.

J. So come while sheep, now shorn, may run
Clean white, below the yellow sun,
In daisy beds ; before
The swinging hook may come to shear
The yellow wheat with nodding ear,
Come, welcome, to my door.

F.   I'll rest
Beside the clover-whiten'd knap,
With weary hand upon my lap,
One day your happy guest.

HOME'S A NEST

A Father (*F.*) and a Neighbour or Chorus of Neighbours (*C.*)

F. HERE under the porch's grey bow,
All my children have shot to and fro,
With a sleek little head.

C.   Home's a nest.

F. Here are windows where hills, in the blue
Of the sky, so long shone to their view,
And the sun's evening red—darted in,
And the nooks where their toetips all sprang,
And the walls and the places that rang
With their high-screaming din.

C.   Home's a nest ;
O home is a nest of the spring,
Where children may grow to take wing.

F. As small-footed maidens here walk'd
    By their mother, their little tongues talk'd
    To her downlooking face.

C.   Home's a nest.

F. And the boys trotted on at my side,
    With the two-steps they put to one stride
    Of my big-footed pace :—and now each
    Is withdrawn from our side and our hand,
    And the oldest as far as the land
    Of old England may reach.

C.   Home's a nest;
    A nest where the young folk are bred
    Up, to take on the work of the dead.

F. And here, when the boys had begun
    At their sisters with bantering fun,
    How brisk was each tongue

C.   Home's a nest.

F. Of the girls, who could very soon find
How to pay off their brothers in kind,
Whether older or young,—and now each
Has his own day of life, and his door,
While his words and his doings no more
To the others may reach.

C. Home's a nest,
Where babes may grow women and men,
For the rearing of children again.

F. There straight-gaited John, that can show
How to handle a sword with a foe,
Is a comely young man ;

C. Home's a nest.

F. And he swings a good blade by a hand
That has hit a few blows for his land.
And the merry-soul'd Ann ;—oh ! a dear,
She is wedded, and taken to turn
Her own cheeses, and roll her own churn,
But a good way from here.

C.   Home's a nest,
Where our children grow up to take on
Our own places, when we are all gone.

F. There is dapper young Joe, that has made
A good jobbing in cattle, his trade,
Is so skilful of mind,
C.   Home's a nest,

F. That the while any bullock might blare,
He would know her all round, ev'ry hair;
And my Fanny, so kind—and so mild,
That I often would hope she might stay
At my hearth, she is taken away,
Ay, my Fanny, dear child!
C.   Home's a nest,
All forsaken, when children have flown,
Like a nest in bush-top alone.

F. There is Jim, that the neighbours all round
Made their pet, is now gone, and is bound
To a very good trade.

C.   Home's a nest.

F. Though his head is as thoughtless, a lout,

As the ball he would hit so about,

In the games that they play'd,—and he's near;

But my Willie is gone from my door,

And too far to come back any more,

Any more to come here.

C.   Home's a nest,

Where our children are bred to fulfil

Not our own, but our Father's good will.

ON THE ROAD

STILL green on the limbs of the oak were the leaves,
Where the sloe daily grew, with its skin-bloom of grey,
Though in fields, summer-burnt, stood the bent-grass,
    well brown'd,
And the stubble of wheatfields was withering white,
While sooner the sunlight now sank from the sight,
And longer now linger'd the dim-roaded night.

But bright was the daylight that dried up the dew,
As the foam-water fill'd the wide pool in its fall,
And as I came to climb, by the chalk of the cliff,
The white road full steep to the wayfaring step,
Where along by the hill, with a high-beating breast,
Went the girl or the man to the feast in their best.

There the horse would prance by, with his neck a
  high bow,
And would toss up his nose over outspringing knees ;
And the ox, with sleek hide, and with low-swimming
  head ;
And the sheep, little kneed, with a quickdipping nod;
And a girl, with her head carried on in a proud
Gait of walking, as smooth as an air-swimming cloud.

MOTHER OF MOTHERS

By summer and fall, and by tide upon tide,
The apple-tree stems may lean lower aside,
And the loosening bricks, out in orchard, may fall
Cn the tree-begloom'd grass, from the long-sided wall,
And the bank-sweeping water, with shock upon shock,
May wash down the tongue of dry ground at the rock;

    And old folks, once gay

      And sprightly of limb,

      With eyes wearing dim,

    May now stoop on their way.

There's an old leaning stone in the churchyard,
    bespread
With the scales of grey lichen above a green bed,

With the name of a mother that few or that none
Now alive e'er beheld by the light of the sun—
Aye, a mother of mothers, from older to young,
To the mother that worded my own little tongue,

    And found the wall sound,

      And apple-trees trim,

      And play'd on the brim

    That is wash'd from the ground.

Oh ! now could she come, as we all have been told
She walk'd in her time, of the comeliest mould,
And show us, as what we may see in a dream,
Her looks and her smiles by the twilighted stream,
Where star-beams may twinkle through leaves of
    the oak,
And tell us her tales of her old fellow folk

    That here have liv'd on,

      In joy or in woe,

      From sprightly to slow,

    And from blooming to wan.

K

What maid was belov'd or what woman was bride,

Who droop'd in their grief or upstraighten'd with pride,

Who knelt in the church, putting head beside head,

Who stood to the children or mourn'd for the dead,

Who milk'd at the dairy in long-shaded light,

Who knelt up to thatch the round rick's peakèd height,

What mower was strong,

Or what haymaker quick,

Who play'd the best trick,

Or who sang the best song.

FALLING THINGS

IN THEIR SEASONS.

In sunny time, when people pass
By leafy trees and flow'ry grass,
And swallows' wings, with sweeping tips,
O'ershoot the streams in swinging dips,
And pale-green scales of elm-trees strew
The road below the dusty shoe,

    When bloom of May,
      In scales of white,
      May whirl their flight
    By lambs at play,
      Then we awhile,
      By path and stile,
      May stroll a mile
    Where Stour may stray.

In fall, when ash-tree keys fly free,
To whirl below their mother tree,
Or wingèd pods, from time to time,
Fly spinning off the spreading lime ;
Or thistledown is rolling light,
To pitch and rise in fitful flight ;
    When leaves offshed
        From yellow boughs,
        Pitch down by cows
    Of yellow red,
        Where Stour may wind ;
        We still shall find
        A joy of mind
    Above its bed.

And there's a tide, when rain will fall
From dripping eaves of rick or stall,
Or snow-flakes, whirling down, may roll
From windy bank to windless hole,

And tip the post with ice, and fill,

With icy dust the road up hill;

    When storms fly dark,

      Or patt'ring hail

      May beat the rail,

    Or trees' wet bark ;

      And then, through all

      That there may fall,

      I'll come and call

    By Woodcombe Park.

THE MORNING MOON

'TWAS when the op'ning dawn was still,
I took my lonely road, up hill,
Toward the eastern sky, in gloom,
Or touch'd with palest primrose bloom;
And there the moon, at morning break,
Though yet unset, was gleaming weak,
And fresh'ning air began to pass,
All voiceless, over darksome grass,

> Before the sun
> Had yet begun

To dazzle down the morning moon.

By Maycreech hillock lay the cows,

Below the ash-trees' nodding boughs,

And water fell, from block to block

Of mossy stone, down Bu¬ncleeve rock,

By poplar-trees that stood, as slim

'S a feather, by the stream's green brim;

And down about the mill, that stood

Half darken'd off below the wood,

   The rambling brook,

   From nook to nook,

Flow'd on below the morning moon.

At mother's house I made a stand,

Where no one stirr'd with foot or hand;

No smoke above the chimney reek'd,

No winch above the well-mouth creak'd;

No casement open'd out, to catch

The air below the eaves of thatch;

Nor down before her cleanly floor
Had open'd back her heavy door;
And there the hatch,
With fasten'd latch,
Stood close, below the morning moon:

And she, dear soul, so good and kind,
Had holden long, in my young mind
Of holy thoughts, the highest place
Of honour, for her love and grace.
But now my wife, to heart and sight,
May seem to shine a fuller light;
And as the sun may rise to view,
To dim the moon, from pale to blue,
My comely bride
May seem to hide
My mother, now my morning moon.

But still 'tis wrong that men should slight,
By day, the midnight's weaker light,

That show'd them, though its gleams were dim,

Where roads had risk of life or limb;

And though the day my wife has made

May shine in joy without a shade,

So long 's my life shall hold in flight,

By sunsped day and moonskied night,

    Still never let

    My heart forget

My mother, now my morning moon.

JOY PASSING BY

When ice all melted to the sun,
And left the wavy streams to run,
We long'd, as summer came, to roll
In river foam, o'er depth and shoal;
And if we lost our loose-bow'd swing,
We had a kite to pull our string;
    Or, if no ball
    Would rise or fall
With us, another joy was nigh
Before our joy all pass'd us by.

If leaves of trees, that wind stripp'd bare
At morning, fly on evening air,
We still look on for summer boughs
To shade again our sunburnt brows,

Where orchard blooms' white scales may fall,
May hang the apple's blushing ball.

New hopes come on

For old ones gone,
As day on day may shine on high,
Until our joys all pass us by.

My childhood yearn'd to reach the span
Of boyhood's life, and be a man;
And then I look'd, in manhood's pride,
For manhood's sweetest choice, a bride;
And then to lovely children, come ·
To make my home a dearer home.

But now my mind

Can look behind
For joy, and wonder, with a sigh,
When all my joys have pass'd me by.

Was it when once I miss'd a call
To rise, and thenceforth seem'd to fall,

Or when my wife to my hands left
Her few bright keys, a doleful heft,
Or when before the door I stood
To watch a child away for good,

    Or where some crowd
    In mirth was loud,

Or where I saw a mourner sigh,
Where did my joy all pass me by.

RIGHTING UP THE CHURCH

BRIGHT was the morning and bright was the moon,
Bright was the forenoon and bright was the noon,
Bright was the road down the sunshiny ridge,
Bright was the water and bright was the bridge;
Bright in the light were two eyes in my sight,
On the road that I took up to Brenbury Tow'r:
The eyes at my side were my Fanny's, my bride,
The day of my wedding, my wedding's gay hour;
So, if you have work in the church to make good,
Here's my bit of silver to buy stone or wood.

Here we took up our child, to be bound by a vow

To his Saviour, and mark'd with the cross on his brow:

While his soft little face, and two hands, were in sight,

But the rest of his shape under long folds of white,

And with little blue eyes, to the blue of the skies;

There blinking, look'd upward our dear little boy

That his mother would call, while he'd no name at all,

Her 'Dear' and her 'Pretty,' her 'Love' and her 'Joy':

So, if you would put the old building to rights,

I will pay for a stroke—you shall have my two mites.

·

JOHN TALKING ANGRILY

OF A NEIGHBOUR BEFORE AN ECHO

WHO is he? I should like to be told;

What is he? I should wish him to show;

Why the Brines' name will stand good for gold,

While the Browns are a set that none know.

> *Echo.* No, no.

No, I'm not asham'd of my place;

No, I'm not asham'd of my name;

No, I can well hold up my face,

While he must hang his down for shame.

> *Echo.* For shame!

Since now he bestrides an old mare,

His lips, O with pride how they pout !

Though his feet once trudged about bare,

When I had a horse to ride out.

Echo. I doubt.

No, he's not too safe from a fall:

If a half I am told is but true,

I could very soon make him look small,

With a turn I could very well do.

Echo. Well do.

His pride would have come to an end

Long ago, as it must bye-and-bye,

If I had not stood for his friend

As I did, and the greater oaf I.

Echo. O fie !

I may be a little foreright,

But I never would do on the sly

Little doings, not fit for the light;

You will never find me in a lie.

Echo. A lie.

THE SHOP OF MEAT-WARE

OR

WARES TO EAT

(The complaint of a housemother who keeps
a huxter's shop)

By selling meat-ware I shall get no meat;

I must not keep a shop of wares to eat.

I have some goods, but I can hardly think

That they are sold as quickly as they shrink;

I have some goods, but yet my little stocks

Will waste away, like camphor in a box.

Some hand, at whiles, steals in, and slily slips

Some little thing away for some two lips.

You people here don't wait for gain of trade,

But take the store before the gain is made.

I had some eggs, and I can miss some eggs,

And I don't think they went without some legs.

I had some eggs, and some have left my store,

And I don't think they travell'd out of door ;

I had some eggs, and eggs have gone from hence,

And I don't think they brought me any pence ;

I had some eggs, as yet I know full well ;

I bought some eggs, but now have none to sell.

WALKING HOME AT NIGHT

HUSBAND TO WIFE

You then for me made up your mind
To leave your rights of home behind.
Your width of table-rim, and space
Of fireside floor, your sitting-place,
And all your claim to share the best,
Of all the house, with all the rest,
To guide for me, my house, and all
My home, though small my home may be.

Come, hood your head ; the wind is keen.
Come this side—here : I'll be your screen.

The clothes your mother put you on
Are quite outworn and wholly gone,

And now you wear, from crown to shoe,
What my true love has bought you new,
That now, in comely shape, is shown,
My own will's gift, to deck my own;
And oh! of all I have to share,
For your true share a half is small.

Come, hood your head; wrap up, now do.
Walk close to me : I'll shelter you.

And now, when we go out to spend
A frosty night with some old friend,
And ringing clocks may tell, at last,
The evening hours have fled too fast,
No forkèd roads, to left and right,
Will sunder us, for night or light;
But all my woe 's for you to feel,
And all my weal 's for you to know.

Come hood your head. You can't see out?
I'll lead you right, you need not doubt.

THE KNOLL

(The speaker, who lives by the knoll, talks to an old friend)

O HOME, people tell us, is home
          be it never so homely,
And Meldon 's the home where my fathers
          all sleep by the knoll.

And there they have left me a living,
          in land, where, in summer,
My hay, wither'd grey, awaits hauling
          in heap, by the knoll.

And there, among bright-shining grass-blades,
          and bent-grass, in autumn,
My cows may all lie near the waters
          that creep by the knoll,

And up on the slope of the hillocks,
      by white-rinded ash-trees,
Are ledges of grass and of thyme-beds,
      with sheep, by the knoll.

And down on the west of my house
      is a rookery, rocking
In trees that will ward off the winds
      that may sweep by the knoll.

And there I have windows outlooking
      to blushing-skied sunset,
And others that face the fresh morning's
      first peep, by the knoll.

And though there is no place but heaven
      without any sorrow,
And I, like my fellows in trial,
      may weep by the knoll,

Still, while I fulfil, like a hireling,
      the day of my labour,
I wish, if my wish is not sinful,
      to keep by the knoll.

So, if you can find a day empty
      of work, with fine weather,
And feel yourself willing to climb
      up the steep by the knoll,

Come up, and we'll make ourselves merry
      once more, all together;
You'll find that your bed and your board
      shall be cheap by the knoll.

A WISH FULFILLED

My longing wishes, wand'ring wild
　Beyond the good I had,
Would hang on other gifts, that pride
　Might turn from good to bad;
And in my dream, I still would hope
For this green slope, where now the stream
Or gives, or takes, with rambling flight,
My jutting land, on left or right,
　By dipping downs, at dawn of day,
　Or dewy dells, when daylight dies.

And I have lofty trees to sway,
　Where western wind may roar
Against their bowing heads, to play
　The softer round my door,

As on they pass, and chase the flight
Of running light, on shaded grass,
And sweep along the· shaken sedge,
And rustle by the dead-leav'd hedge,
　By morning meads, or mid-day mound,
　Or mellow midnight's mounted moon.

And there two cows with wide-horn'd head
　Now stalk, onstepping slow,　　·
And one is dun, and one is red
　With face as white as snow;
And there, full wide of back, 's my mare,
For some long pair of legs to stride,
A cunning jade, that now would find
Out all my roads if I were blind,
　By winding ways, on-wand'ring wide,
　Or wilder waste, or wind-blown wood.

And when my work has brought me all

   Its earnings, day by day,

And I have paid each man his call

   On me for lawful pay,

I still can spare enough to grant

My wife a jaunt, with weather fair,

Or buy my boy a taking toy,

Or make a doll my daughter's joy,

   With limber limbs all lopping loose

   Or leaning low in little laps.

AT THE DOOR

The waters roll, quick-bubbling by the shoal,
  Or leap the rock, outfoaming in a bow.
The wind blows free in gushes round the tree,
  Along the grove of oaks in double row,
Where lovers seek the maidens' evening floor,
With stip-step light, and tip-tap slight,
         Against the door.

With iron bound, the wheel-rims roll around,
  And crunch the crackling flint below their load.
The gravel, trod by horses ironshod,
  All crackles shrill along the beaten road,

Where lovers come to seek, in our old place,
With stip-step light, and tip-tap slight, .
        The maiden's face.

And oh ! how sweet's the time the lover's feet
    May come before the door to seek a bride,
As he may stand and knock with shaking hand,
    And lean to hear the sweetest voice inside ;
While 'there a heart will leap, to hear once more
The stip-step light, and tip-tap slight,
        Against the door.

How sweet's the time when we are in our prime,
    With children, now our care and aye our joy,
And child by child may scamper, skipping wild,
    Back home from school or play-games, girl or boy,
And there upon the door-stone leap once more,
With stip-step light, and tip-tap slight,
        Against the door.

Be my abode, beside some uphill road,

    Where people pass along, if not abide,

And not a place where day may bring no face

    With kindly smiles, as lonesome hours may glide;

But let me hear some friend, well-known before,

With stip-step light, and tip-tap slight,

        Against the door.

.

HILL AND DELL

AT John's, up on Sandhills, 'tis healthy and dry,
Though I may not like it, it may be—not I.
Where fir-trees are spindling, with tapering tops,
From leafy-leav'd fern in the cold stunted copse,
And under keen gorsebrakes, all yellow in bloom,
The skylark's brown nest is deep-hidden in gloom ;
And high on the cliff, where no foot ever wore
A path to the threshold, 's the sandmartin's door,
On waterless heights, while the winds lowly sigh,
On tree-climbing ivy, before the blue sky.

I think I could hardly like his place as well
As my own shelter'd home in the timbery dell,

Where rooks come to build in the high-swaying boughs,
And broadheaded oaks yield a shade for the cows ;
Where grey-headed withy-trees lean o'er the brook
Of grey-lighted waters that whirl by the nook,
And only the girls and the swans are in white,
Like snow on grey moss in·the midwinter's light,
And wind softly drives, with a low rustling sound,
By waves on the water and grass on the ground.

DANIEL AND JANE

IN THE PUMP COURT

Daniel (D). Jane (J). Jane's mother (M).

Daniel comes over to Jane's, and while talking, pumps the water over
the trough upon the pavement.

D. HERE ! if I had your trap and beast,

I'd drive you all to Meldon feast.

J. Oh ! very well : but did he find

The pump a plaything to his mind ?

There's Daniel plying all his bones,

In pumping wet about the stones :

And who's to trample, just for sport

To you, about this wat'ry court ?

No, I should only like to shed

The water on your empty head.

M

D. And did the frog, as people say,
    Catch cold of wetted feet, one day?

J. See how his two long armbones sway,
    And how his peakèd elbows play.

D. The pattens. How about a chap
    And pattens, out at Oakrow knap?

J. See how he chuckles. Come, tell out
    What you can find to grin about.

D. We left our pattens, in a stroll
    We lately took, at Oakrow knoll.

J. O! did we? Well, that must be fun,
    With pattens out, and home with none.

D. We call'd to take them, after dark,
    Where William Henstone, with a spark.

Of manhood in his soul, must come
Down Oakrow road, to see us home.

J. Now you be off. I'll souse a bowl
Of buttermilk about your poll.
No, I should have no call for traps,
To catch the very best of chaps.
Not lopping, lolling, long-ear'd louts
Like you.

D.   O no, but *Tommy Touts.*

J. (*slapping his head at every strong sound.*)
Nor drawling, dragging, drowsy drones.
D. But *Tom*, ha ! hah ! *Tom Shaklebones.*

M. Why lauk ! whatever is this row ?
Why Jane, whatever is it now ?

J. Why, Dan is at his sauce again.
D. 'Tis only fun, once now and then.

J. He's here to know if we would ride
    To Meldon feast, this Whitsuntide.

D. Ay, Meldon feast, if you can spare
    Your little waggon, with the mare.

M. O no, you bring us little gains
    When your hand shakes our old mare's reins;
    Last month you beat her steaming hide,
    Till we all thought she must have died,
    Before a load of people, full
    Enough for three such mares to pull;
    A squeezing load of girls and chaps,
    With some almost in others' laps,
    And simpering faces up as thick
    As ever face by face could stick,
    And work'd the mare along as though
    She had but bags of down in tow,
    As you did whip, and whop, and whack
    Her panting sides and steaming back.

D. But now the load would be but small,

    We have no Browns at home to haul,

    And Jane could go with what's his name—

J. Why Dan, you silly chap, for shame !

D. There I would only take a few

    Of your choice, you can tell me who.

M. O, well, then, nobody at all.

J. Hee, heeh ! *D.* Hah, hah ! *J.* Now you sing

    small.

D. I'll drive the Wellburns, they'll be glad

    To have me when I can be had.

HOME

WITH the sun glowing warm at its height,
And the people at work in white sleeves,
And the gold-banded bee in its flight,
With the quick-flitting birds among leaves :
There my two little children would run,
And would reach and would roll in their fun,
And would clasp in their hands,

    Stick or stone for their play,—
In their hands that but little had grown,
For their play, with a stick or a stone.

As the sun from his high summer bow,

To the west of the orchard would fall,

He would leave the brown beehives in row,

In the shade of the houses' grey wall.

And the flowers, outshining in bloom,

Some in light, and some others in gloom,

To the cool of the air,

 And the damp of the dew,—

The air from the apple-tree shades,

And the dew on the grasses' green blades.

And there was my orchard well-tined,

With a hedge, and a steep-sided bank ;

Where ivy had twin'd on the rind

Of the wood-stems, and trees in high rank,

To keep out the wide lippèd cow,

And the stiff-snouted swine that would plough

Up the soft-bladed grass,

 By the young apple-trees—

The grass that had grown a good height,

And the trees that in blossom were white.

O when is a father's good time,

That will yield to his toil the best joy?

Is it when he is spending his prime

For his children, the girl and the boy?

Or when they have grown to their height,

And are gone from his hearing and sight,

And their mother's one voice

    Is left home at the door—

A voice that no longer may sing,

At the door that more seldom may swing?

.

FELLOWSHIP

WELL here, another year, at least,

We go along with blinking sight,

By smoky dust arising white,

Up off our road, to Lincham feast.

With trudging steps of tramping feet,

We souls on foot, with foot-folk meet :

For we that cannot hope to ride

For ease or pride, have fellowship.

And so, good father tried to show

To folk with hands on right or left,

Down-pull'd by some great bundle's heft,

And trudging weary, to or fro :

That rich men are but one to ten
When reckon'd off with working men,
And so have less, the while the poor
Have ten times more of fellowship.

He thought, good man, whatever part
We have to play, we all shall find
That fellowship of kind with kind
Must keep us better up in heart.
And why should working folk be shy
Of work, with mostly work-folk by,
While kings must live in lonesome states
With none for mates in fellowship ? *

* Xenophon, in his *Hiero*, chap. vii., makes the king say to
Simonides :—'I wish to show you those pleasures which I en-
joyed while I was a common man ; and now, since I have been
a king, I feel I have lost. I was then among my fellows, and
happy with them as they were happy with me.'

Tall chimneys up with high-flown larks,
And houses, roods in length, with sights
Of windows glaring off in lights,
That shoot up slopes of wood-bound parks,
Are far and wide, and not so thick
As poor men's little homes of brick,
By ones or twos, or else in row
So small and low, in fellowship.

But we, wherever we may come,
Have fellowship in hands and loads,
And fellowship of feet on roads,
And lowliness of house and home ;
And fellowship in homely fare,
And homely garb for daily wear.
And so may Heaven bless the more
The working poor in fellowship.

AIR AND LIGHT

Ah ! look and see how widely free
   O'er all the land the wind will spread ;
If here a tree-top sways, a tree
   On yonder hillock waves its head.
How wide the light outshows to sight
The place and living face of man ?
How far the river runs for lip
To drink, or hand to sink and dip.

But one may sink with sudden woe
   That may not pass, in wider flight,
To other souls, declining slow,
   And hush'd, like birds at fall of night.

And some are sad, while some are glad ;
In turn we all may mourn our lot:
And days that come in joy may go
In evenings sad with heavy woe.

The morning sun may cast abroad
  His light on dew about our feet,
And down below his noontide road
  The streams may glare below his heat ;
The evening light may sparkle bright
Across the quiv'ring gossamer ;
But I, though fair he still may glow,
Must miss a face he cannot show.

MELDON HILL

I TOOK the road of dusty stone
To walk alone, by Meldon hill,
Along the knap, with woody crown,
That slopes far down, by Meldon Hill;
While sunlight overshot the copse
Of underwood, with brown-twigg'd tops,
By sky-belighted stream and pool,
With eddies cool, by Meldon Hill.

And down below were many sights
Of yellow lights, by Meldon Hill;
The trees above the brindled cows,
With budding boughs, by Meldon Hill;

And bridgèd roads and waterfalls,

And house by house with sunny walls,

And one, where somebody may come

To guide my home, from Meldon Hill.

Whenever I may climb the stiles

Of these two miles, to Meldon Hill,

By elms above the wreathing smoke,

Or lonesome oak, to Meldon Hill,

How much I have to talk about;

But that is what must now come out,

That I've a house, that some sweet bride

Must come to guide, from Meldon Hill.

SOFT SOUNDS

Ah ! then as we might meet, all young,
And trip with nimble feet, abroad,
Or else in knots might come, full gay,
Along the grove up home.
　Sis, sis, the whispers, here and there,
　　Would hiss, from man and maid in pair.

Or when the wind, upspringing keen
From eastern slopes, would fling about
The snow, or overlay the tree
And ground with hoar-frost grey,
　Sis, sis, our nimble steps would sound
　　As we would trip o'er frosty ground.

At times, when leaves were dead, and fell
Down-scatter'd, browny-red ; or spun
In windy rings around our feet,
On timber-shaded ground :
   Sis, sis, our shoes would rustle light
   On leaves and bentgrass, wither'd white.

And when, again, we pass'd along
The half-dried hay all cast abroad,
In air that smelt full sweet, about
Our nimbly-stepping feet :
   Sis, sis, our footsteps on the hay
   Did sound along our summer way.

And still may joy betide us all,
Though scatter'd far and wide away ;
And may we find, by grace, that now,
Wherever be our place,
   Teeh, hee shall be our merry sound
   Along the road or grassy ground.

THE VOICE AT HOME

THOUGH black the winter clouds might rise
    To back the rick's brown tip,
Though dark might reach the leafless hedge,
    And bark of trees might drip,
With health and work and livelihood,
I never pin'd for others' good.

And down along the timber'd grove,
    All brown with leaves long shed,
Where round the ivy-hooded thorn
    The ground was dry to tread,
I then would walk in home, with pride,
On foot, and heedless who might ride.

And come from evening's chilly shades,
  In home, I took, at night,
My place within the settle's back,
  With face in fire-light,
Where one would spread my evening board
With soul-beguiling smile and word.

Then high above the chimney top,
  Might cry the wind, and low
Might sound, beside my window panes,
  And round my porch's bow,
Its sounds that now so sadly moan
Where one sweet voice no more is known.

How sweetly seem'd the running waves
  To meet the mossy rock,
As quickly-flapping flames might play
  By tickings of the clock ;
But now their sounds are sad to hear,
Since one sweet tongue no more is near.

THE FIRESIDE CHAIRS

HUSBAND TO WIFE

The daylight gains upon the night,
And birds are out in later flight;
'Tis cold enough to spread our hands,
Once now and then, to glowing brands.
So now we two are here alone
To make a quiet hour our own,
We'll take, with face to face, once more
Our places on the warm hearth floor,
Where you shall have the window view
Outside, and I can look on you.

When first I brought you home, my bride,

In yellow glow of summer tide,

I wanted you to take a chair

On that side of the fire—out there—

And have the ground and sky in sight,

With face against the window light;

While I, back here, should have my brow

In shade, and sit where I am now;

That you might see the land outside,

And I might look on you, my bride.

And there the gliding waters spread,

By waving elm-trees over head,

Below the hill that slopes above

The path, along the high-treed grove,

Where sighing winds once whisper'd down

Our whisper'd words; and there's the crown

Of *Duncliffe* hill, where widening shades

Of timber fall on sloping glades:

So you enjoy the green and blue

Without, and I will look on you.

And there we pull'd, within the copse,

With nutting-crooks the hazel tops,

That now arise, unleaved and black,

Too thin to keep the wind-blast back ;

And there's the church, and spreading lime,

Where we did meet at evening time,

In clusters, on the beaten green,

In glee, to see and to be seen ;

All old sights, welcomer than new,

And look'd on, as I look'd on you.

COME AND MEET ME

HUSBAND TO WIFE

WELL, to day, then, I shall roll off on the road
Round by Woodcombe, out to Shellbrook, to the mill ;
With my brand-new little spring-cart, with a load,
To come loadless round by Chalk-hill, at my will :
As the whole day will be dry,
By the tokens of the sky,
Come to meet me, with the children, on the road.

For the sunshine, from the blue sky's hollow height,
Now is glitt'ring on the stream-wave, and the sedge ;
And the orchard is a broad sheet of the white
Of new blossom, over blossom on the hedge :

So when clock-bells ring out four,

Let them send you out of door,

Come to meet me, with the children, on the road.

You can saunter, if I'm lated by the clock,

To some blue-bells, for the children, on the ridge;

Or can loiter by the tree-shades, on the rock

Where the water tumbles headlong by the bridge :

While the boy's line and his hook

May catch minnows in the brook,

Out to meet me, with his sister, on the road.

You may dawdle, for a furlong on a-head,

And be welcome at the Weldons, on the knap,

Where the cowslips are so close grown in a bed,

That our Poll's hands will have soon fill'd up her lap,

For a toss-ball, up as big

As her small head's curly wig,

Out to meet me, with her brother, on the road.

At the time, then, I have told you, you may hear

My two wheel-rims and four horse-shoes on the road,

And the spring-cart with the seat up, near and near,

To spin you home, with the children, for its load.

So come out, then, to the sun,

With the children, for a run :

Come and meet me, with the children, on the road.

MY FORE-ELDERS

When from the child that still is led
By hand, a father's hand is gone—
Or when a few-year'd mother, dead,
Has left her children, growing on—
When men have left their children staid,
And they again have boy and maid—
Oh ! can they know, as years máy roll,
Their children's children, soul by soul.
If this, with souls in Heav'n, can be,
Do my fore-elders know of me ?

My elders' elders, man and wife,
Were borne full early to the tomb,
With children, still in childhood life,
To play with butterfly or bloom.

And did they see the seasons mould

Their faces on, from young to old;

As years might bring them, turn by turn,

A time to laugh or time to mourn.

If this with souls in Heav'n can be,

Do my fore-elders know of me?

How fain I now would walk the floor

Within their mossy porch's bow,

Or linger by their church's door,

Or road that bore them to and fro,

Or nook where once they built their mow,

Or gateway open to their plough—

Though now, indeed, no gate is swung,

That their live hands had ever hung—

If I could know that they would see

Their child's late child, and know of me.

THE LOST LITTLE SISTER

On summer nights, as day did gleam,
With waning light, from red to wan,
And we did play above the stream,
That near our house-lawn rambled on,
Our little sister lightly flew
And skipp'd about, in all her pride
Of snow-white frock and sash of blue,
A shape that night was slow to hide—
Beside the brook, that trickled thin
Among the pebbles, out and in.

When wind may blow, at evening-tide,
Now here, now there, by mound and nook,
It may be on the leafy lime,
Or grey-bough'd withy by the brook,

Or on the apple-trees may fall,

Or on the elms, beside the grove,

Or on the lofty tower's wall,

On places where we used to rove—

Then ev'ry sound, in ev'ry place,

Will call to mind her pretty face.

Where periwinkle's buds of blue,

By lilies' hollow cups may wind,

What, then, can their two colours do,

But call our sister back to mind ?

She wore no black—she wore her white,

She wore no black—she wore her blue.

She never mourn'd another's flight,

For she has been the first that flew,

From where our nimble feet did tread,

From stone to stone, the water's bed.

BLACK AND WHITE

By the wall of the garden that glimmer'd, chalk white,

In the light of the moon, back in May,

There were you all in black, at my side, coming round

On the ground where the cypress did sway :

Oh ! the white and the black. Which was fairest to
    view ?

Why the black, become fairest on you.

By the water downfalling in many a bow,

White as snow, on the rock's peaky steep ;

There your own petted cow show'd the ridge of her back,

Of deep black, as she lay for her sleep :

Oh ! the white and the black. Which was fairest to
    view ?

Why the black, become fairest on you.

When you stroll'd down the village at evening, bedight

All in white, in the warm summer-tide,

The while *Towsy*, your loving old dog, with his back

Sleeky black, trotted on at your side :

Ah ! the black and the white.   Which was fairest to
view ?

Why the white, become fairest on you.

At the end of the barton the granary stood,

Of black wood, with white geese at its side;

And the white-wingèd swans, on the quick-running wave,

By the cave of black darkness did glide :

Oh ! the black and the white.   Which was fairest to
view ?

Why the white, become fairest on you.

BED-RIDDEN

THE sun may in glory go by,

   Though by cloudiness hidden from sight;

And the moon may be bright in the sky,

   Though an air-mist may smother its light.

There is joy in the world among some,

   And among them may joy ever be;

And oh ! is there health-joy to come,

   Come any more unto me ?

The stream may be running its way,

   Under ice that lies dead as the stone,

And below the dark water may play

   The quick fishes in swimmings unshown,

There is sprightliness shown among some,

    Aye, and sprightly may they ever be,

And oh! is there limb-strength to come,

    Come any more unto me?

THE WINDOW

(Grounded on a Neapolitan ballad, 'Fenesta che lucive
e mo non luce.')

BROTHER AND SISTER

B. HERE come I back, and find her window fast
And faceless. Sister, can she be unwell ?

S. O brother, 'tis a heavy truth to tell,
Your Jessie has been ill. Her days are past.
Forego your hope to take her to your side,
She could not linger here to be your bride.

B. Oh ! Sister dear, whatever are your words !
Dear sister, oh ! whatever do you say !

S. If you believe me not, behold the day,
How downcast are its clouds, how still its birds :
O no, I tell you only what is true,
The house can show no Jessie Dean to you.

B. O Jessie Dean, and thou art dead, art gone,

Thy eyes now closed, shall look no more on me,

But thou to mine art ever fair to see ;

As I have loved thee, I shall love thee on,

And oh ! how willingly could I have died,

And gone at once to slumber by thy side.

Farewell, dear window.   Now be shut all day,

Since Jessie sits no more behind thy glass :

And I, below thee, now no more will pass,

But henceforth go along the churchyard way,

Till I myself be called at last to share

The angel life of Jessie, angel fair.

PLORATA VERIS LACHRYMIS

O NOW, my true and dearest bride,
Since thou hast left my lonely side,
My life has lost its hope and zest.
The sun rolls on from east to west,
But brings no more that evening rest,
Thy loving-kindness made so sweet,
And time is slow that once was fleet,
          As day by day was waning.

The last sad day that show'd thee lain
Before me, smiling in thy pain,
The sun soar'd high along his way
To mark the longest summer day,
And show to me the latest play

Of thy sweet smile, and thence, as all

The days' lengths shrunk from small to small,

My joy began its waning.

And now 'tis keenest pain to see

Whate'er I saw in bliss with thee.

The softest airs that ever blow,

The fairest days that ever glow,

Unfelt by thee, but bring me woe.

And sorrowful I kneel in pray'r,

Which thou no longer, now, canst share,

As day by day is waning.

How can I live my lonesome days?

How can I tread my lonesome ways?

How can I take my lonesome meal?

Or how outlive the grief I feel?

Or how again look on to weal?

Or sit, at rest, before the heat

Of winter fires, to miss thy feet,

When evening light is waning.

Thy voice is still I lov'd to hear,

Thy voice is lost I held so dear.

Since death unlocks thy hand from mine,

No love awaits me such as thine ;

Oh ! boon the hardest to resign !

But if we meet again at last

In heav'n, I little care how fast

My life may now be waning.

DO GOOD

AH ! child ! the stream that brings
   To thirsty lips their drink,
Is seldom drain'd ; for springs
   Pour water to its brink.

The wellsprings that supply
   The streams, are seldom spent,
For clouds of rain come by
   To pay them what they lent.

The clouds that cast their rain
   On lands that yield our food,
Have water from the main,
   To make their losses good.

The sea is paid by lands,
    With streams from ev'ry shore;
So give with kindly hands,
    For God can give you more.

He would that in a ring
    His blessings should be sent,
From living thing to thing,
    But nowhere staid or spent.

And ev'ry soul that takes,
    But yields not on again,
Is so a link that breaks
    In Heaven's love-made chain.

LONDON: PRINTED BY
SPOTTISWOODE AND CO., NEW-STREET SQUARE
AND PARLIAMENT STREET